THOMAS & FRIENDS
MARVELOUS ·MACHINERY·

By Christy Webster
Based on an episode written by Paul Larson and Laura Beaumont

A Random House PICTUREBACK® Book

Random House New York

Thomas the Tank Engine & Friends™

CREATED BY BRITT ALLCROFT

Based on The Railway Series by The Reverend W Awdry.
© 2020 Gullane (Thomas) Limited.
Thomas the Tank Engine & Friends and Thomas & Friends are trademarks of Gullane (Thomas) Limited. © HIT Entertainment Limited.
HIT and the HIT logo are trademarks of HIT Entertainment Limited. Published in the United States by Random House Children's Books,
a division of Penguin Random House LLC, 1745 Broadway, New York, NY 10019, and in Canada by Penguin Random House Canada
Limited, Toronto. Pictureback, Random House, and the Random House colophon are registered trademarks of
Penguin Random House LLC.
ISBN 978-0-593-12763-6
rhcbooks.com   www.thomasandfriends.com
Printed in the United States of America   10 9 8 7 6 5 4 3 2 1

One beautiful, sunny day on the Island of Sodor,
Thomas was puffing along his branch line when he
saw something sleek and shiny flying through the
sky. It looked like a spaceship!

Thomas followed the strange object until it landed at Ulfstead Castle. The Earl came out of the flying machine with his friend Ruth. She had built the flying machine herself! She called it a roadplane.

The Earl and Ruth were planning a technology fair, showcasing lots of new inventions, for the next day. They would need all the engines to help with deliveries.

That night, Thomas and his friends talked about the new inventions. There were robots and flying cars, rockets and submarines. But Thomas was worried. What if the new inventions were so useful that people wouldn't need engines anymore?

The next day, the engines got to work. Percy would deliver tents, Nia would deliver the Ferris wheel, and Thomas would deliver the workers. But on his way, Thomas saw that Nia had derailed!

Thomas knew they needed to get a crane to help. "I'll find Harvey for you," he said.

Percy picked up the tents, but got distracted when Ruth's roadplane flew by. He crashed into Edward!

Thomas knew they needed a large breakdown crane. "I'll find Rocky for you," Thomas said, hoping he would still have time to deliver the workers to the fair.

Thomas sped to the docks to find Rocky. But Thomas was going so fast, he crashed into some trucks, knocking the cargo everywhere.

Now the whole day would be delayed.

Sir Topham Hatt had a talk with the engines. "We will have to work extra hard to get the fair ready in time," he said. "You know what to do."

The engines got back to work.

After dropping off the workers, Thomas had
one more delivery to make. It was a big jet engine!
A professor was trying to get it to work.

Suddenly, the professor pressed the wrong button.
The jet engine roared to life and took off like a rocket
along the tracks.

"Help!" the professor cried.

Thomas raced after it as fast as he could.

Thomas took a shortcut and slipped in front of the jet engine. He slowed it down so the professor could turn it off.

"Thomas is one brave engine," the professor said. "He saved the day!"

"I can see why they gave you the number
one," Ruth said. "You're Really Useful!" Ruth told
Thomas that the steam engine had always been
one of her favorite inventions.

"I'm an invention?" Thomas asked, amazed.

"One of the best inventions ever!" Ruth said.

"You run a great railway, which has earned you this award," the Queen said to Sir Topham Hatt.

Then the Prince gave Thomas a special award, too.

"Thomas, today you are a Royally Useful Engine!" the Queen declared.

"*Peep! Peep!*" Thomas chuffed.

Once they were in the station, Thomas found out who was in Duchess's coach—it was the Queen and the Prince! The Queen was so pleased with Thomas and Sir Topham Hatt, she wanted to give him his award right away.

Duchess and her coaches were heavy, but
Thomas did his best. "Little engines can do big
things!" he said. Duchess agreed. Thomas pushed
her all the way to London, arriving just in time.

Thomas chugged along, but then he saw
Duchess stopped on the track.

"It's my safety valve," Duchess said. "I'll never
get to London on time."

She and Thomas agreed on a plan—he would
push her, and she would show him the way.

Thomas and Sir Topham Hatt were in such a hurry,
they accidentally left their coal stoker behind! Sir Topham
Hatt volunteered to help the Driver shovel coal.

"But, Sir, you'll get dirty!" Thomas protested.

"Sometimes running a railway means getting your
hands dirty," Sir Topham Hatt said.

At the next station, Thomas stopped at the Washdown. There he met an engine named Duchess, who was also running late. Thomas let her use the Washdown first. By the time she was done, it was out of water! Thomas didn't have time to wait. He sped down the line.

Finally Thomas found the right track. But then another engine sped by, spraying mud all over Thomas and Sir Topham Hatt!

Thomas had never been to London before. But he thought he knew the way.

Soon Thomas was lost in a dark forest. The branches scratched his paint.

Sir Topham Hatt was all set for the trip, too.
He wore his best suit and hat.

The young Prince requested that Thomas be the engine to bring Sir Topham Hatt to London. Thomas was so proud. He was cleaned and was all set for the trip.

One evening, Percy was late delivering a very special letter to Sir Topham Hatt. The Queen had invited him to London so she could give him an award for his work on the railway!

By Christy Webster
Based on an episode written by Michael White

A Random House PICTUREBACK® Book

Random House  **New York**

Thomas the Tank Engine & Friends™

CREATED BY BRITT ALLCROFT

Based on The Railway Series by The Reverend W Awdry.
© 2020 Gullane (Thomas) Limited.
Thomas the Tank Engine & Friends and Thomas & Friends are trademarks of Gullane (Thomas) Limited. © HIT Entertainment Limited.
HIT and the HIT logo are trademarks of HIT Entertainment Limited. Published in the United States by Random House Children's Books,
a division of Penguin Random House LLC, 1745 Broadway, New York, NY 10019, and in Canada by Penguin Random House Canada
Limited, Toronto. Pictureback, Random House, and the Random House colophon are registered trademarks of
Penguin Random House LLC.
ISBN 978-0-593-12763-6
rhcbooks.com   www.thomasandfriends.com
Printed in the United States of America 10 9 8 7 6 5 4 3 2 1